Dear Parent:
Your child's love of reading starts here!

Every child learns to read in a different way and at his or her own speed. Some go back and forth between reading levels and read favorite books again and again. Others read through each level in order. You can help your young reader improve and become more confident by encouraging his or her own interests and abilities. From books your child reads with you to the first books he or she reads alone, there are I Can Read Books for every stage of reading:

SHARED READING
Basic language, word repetition, and whimsical illustrations, ideal for sharing with your emergent reader

BEGINNING READING
Short sentences, familiar words, and simple concepts for children eager to read on their own

READING WITH HELP
Engaging stories, longer sentences, and language play for developing readers

READING ALONE
Complex plots, challenging vocabulary, and high-interest topics for the independent reader

ADVANCED READING
Short paragraphs, chapters, and exciting themes for the perfect bridge to chapter books

I Can Read Books have introduced children to the joy of reading since 1957. Featuring award-winning authors and illustrators and a fabulous cast of beloved characters, I Can Read Books set the standard for beginning readers.

A lifetime of discovery begins with the magical words **"I Can Read!"**

Visit www.icanread.com for information
on enriching your child's reading experience.

I Can Read Book® is a trademark of HarperCollins Publishers.

Copyright © by James Dean (for the character of Pete the Cat)
Pete the Cat and the Bad Banana
www.icanread.com
Library of Congress catalog card number: 2013943879
ISBN 978-0-06-230383-7 (trade bdg.)—ISBN 978-0-06-230382-0 (pbk.)

15 16 17 18 PC/WOR   10 9 8 7 6 5 4 3   ❖   First Edition

Pete the Cat
AND THE BAD BANANA

By James Dean

HARPER
An Imprint of HarperCollinsPublishers

Pete the Cat is eating
a banana.

Pete loves bananas.

They are sweet and tasty
and easy to peel.

Every morning, Pete puts
a banana in his cereal.

Sometimes Pete puts
a banana on his
peanut butter sandwich.

But one day,

Pete eats a bad banana.

The banana is gross.

The banana is mushy.

The banana is yucky.

Pete's tummy hurts.

"I will not eat bananas again,"
Pete tells his mom.

Pete's mom tries to help.
She bakes Pete's favorite:
banana bread.

Pete will not touch it.

She makes Pete
a banana cream pie.

Pete will not eat it.

She gets Pete

a big banana split.

"No thanks," Pete says.

Instead, Pete tries a lemon.

It is yellow like a banana.

Pete tastes it.

"Yuck!" says Pete.

The lemon is sour.

Pete tries a pickle.

It is long like a banana.

Pete tastes it.

"Better," Pete says,

"but not as good as a banana."

Pete tries an orange.
It has to be peeled
like a banana.

The orange is sweet,
but it is too juicy.
It makes Pete's paws sticky.

Pete tries fish, plums, rice,
hot dogs, watermelon,
and his mom's nut bread.

Pete eats them all!
He is not hungry
for bananas anymore.

Then comes the big race.
What should Pete have
for breakfast?

A pickle?

No, Pete doesn't eat

pickles for breakfast!

A hot dog?

No, Pete just had a hot dog
for dinner last night.

A lemon?

No. That's just silly.

Pete wants a banana.

They're yummy and healthy.

Bananas are the best!

"Do you have another banana?"
Pete asks.

"Of course," says Greg the Monkey.

START

Pete peels the banana slowly.

It is not brown.

It is not mushy.

Pete takes a teeny, tiny bite.

It is a yummy banana.

It is the best banana ever!

Thanks to Greg and his banana,
Pete wins the race.
Pete is bananas for bananas!

LITTLE HOUSE
Laura Ingalls Wilder

MY FIRST LITTLE HOUSE BOOKS

PRAIRIE
DAY

ADAPTED FROM THE LITTLE HOUSE BOOKS

By Laura Ingalls Wilder

Illustrated by Renée Graef

HARPERCOLLINS PUBLISHERS

For Maxfield
—R.G.

Illustrations prepared with the help of Cathy Holly.

Prairie Day Text adapted from Little House on the Prairie text copyright 1935, copyright renewed 1963, Roger Lea MacBride. Illustrations copyright © 1997 by Renée Graef
Printed in the U.S.A.   All rights reserved.   Library of Congress Cataloging-in-Publication Data   Wilder, Laura Ingalls, 1867–1957.   Prairie day / adapted from the Little
house books by Laura Ingalls Wilder ; illustrated by Renée Graef.   p.   cm. — (My first little house books)   Summary: A little girl and her pioneer family travel
westward to find a new home on the prairie.   ISBN 0-06-025905-1. — ISBN 0-06-025906-X (lib. bdg.)   [1. Frontier and pioneer life—Fiction.   2. Family life—
Fiction.]   I. Graef, Renée, ill.   II. Title.   III. Series.   PZ7.W6461Pr   1997   96-14361   [E]—dc20   CIP AC
1 2 3 4 5 6 7 8 9 10 ❖ First Edition
HarperCollins®, 🏭®, and Little House® are trademarks of HarperCollins Publishers Inc.

Illustrations for the My First Little House Books are inspired by the work of Garth Williams with his permission, which we gratefully acknowledge.

Once upon a time, a little girl named Laura, her Pa and her Ma, her big sister, Mary, her baby sister, Carrie, and their good old bulldog, Jack, headed west in their covered wagon for the prairie.

RICHARD BROTHERS'
GENERAL STORE

They drove through the snowy woods until they came
to the town of Pepin. Pa went inside the store to trade
his furs for things they would need on their journey.
Ma and Laura and Mary ate bread and molasses in
the wagon, and the horses ate corn from nose-bags.

Soon they reached a big lake that stretched flat and smooth and white all the way to the edge of the gray sky.

The horses' hoofs clop-clopped, and the wagon wheels crunched as Pa drove the wagon onto the ice. Laura didn't like it, but she knew nothing could hurt her while Pa and Jack were there.

At last the wagon came to a slope of earth, and there stood a little log house among the trees. It was a tiny house for travelers to camp in. That night Laura and Mary and Ma and Baby Carrie slept in front of the fire, while Pa slept outside to guard the wagon and the horses.

Every day after that they traveled as far as the horses could go, and every night they made camp in a new place. They crossed too many creeks to count and drove across long wooden bridges. They saw strange woods and even stranger country with no trees.

After many days and nights they came to the Kansas prairie, a flat land with rippling grass and a great big sky.

The wind blew Laura's straight brown hair and Mary's golden curls every-which-way.

Soon Laura and Mary were tired of traveling with nothing new to look at. Poor Jack was tired, too. At last Pa stopped the wagon and said, "We'll camp here a day or two." He unharnessed the horses, and they rolled back and forth and over until the feeling of the harness was all gone from their backs.

Pa cleared a space in the prairie grass for a fire, and Laura and Mary helped Ma get supper. Pa brought water from a creek, and Ma mixed the water with cornmeal and salt and patted it into little cakes. She fried slices of fat salt pork in the iron spider. The cakes baked, the meat fried, and Laura grew hungrier and hungrier.

At last supper was ready. Pa and Ma sat on the wagon-seat and Laura and Mary sat on the wagon tongue. Each of them had a tin plate and a steel knife and a steel fork. Ma had a tin cup and Pa had a tin cup, and Baby Carrie had a little one of her own, but Mary and Laura had to share their tin cup.

While they were eating supper, the prairie became dark and still, and soon it was past bedtime. Mary and Laura put their long nightgowns on, said their prayers, and crawled into their little bed in the wagon.

The next morning, they all sat on the clean grass and ate pancakes and bacon and molasses. All around them tiny birds were swinging and singing in tiny voices. "Dickie, dickie," Laura called to them.

"Eat your breakfast, Laura," Ma said. "You must mind your manners, even if we are a hundred miles from anywhere."

After everything in the camp was tidy, Pa went hunting and Laura and Mary went exploring. It was fun to run through the tall grass, in the sunshine and the wind. There were huge rabbits and tiny dickie-birds everywhere, and little brown-striped gophers. Mary and Laura wanted to catch a gopher to take to Ma. Laura ran and ran and couldn't catch one. They took some flowers to Ma instead of a gopher.

Before long, the sun was low, and Pa was coming across the prairie. Laura jumped up and ran to him and hippety-hopped through the tall grass beside him.

That night after supper, Pa's fiddle sang in the starlight. The large bright stars hung down from the sky, and Laura thought the stars might be singing too. Soon it was time for little girls to be in bed, so Ma tied on their nightcaps and tucked them into bed. Tomorrow they must be on their way again to find their new little house on the prairie.